With appreciation for all the teachers who launch readers.
—L.C.

To my wife, PJ, who is out of this world.
—J.L.

10 9 8 7 6 5 4 3 2   19 20 21 22 23
Printed in the U.S.A.   88 • First edition, May 2019

THERE WAS AN OLD ASTRONAUT WHO SWALLOWED THE MOON!

by Lucille Colandro

illustrated by Jared Lee

Cartwheel Books
an imprint of Scholastic Inc.

There was an old astronaut who
swallowed the moon.
I don't know why she swallowed the moon.
It happened at noon.

There was an old astronaut who swallowed a star.
It was bizarre to swallow a star!

She swallowed the star to shoot for the moon.

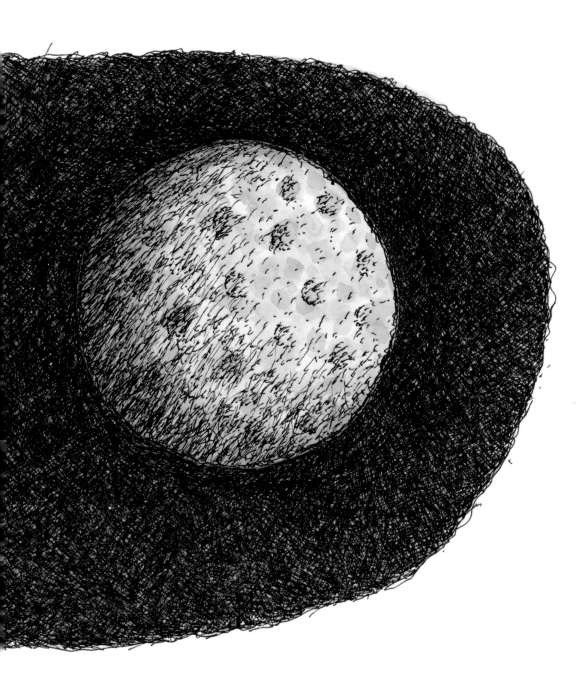

I don't know why she swallowed the moon.
It happened at noon.

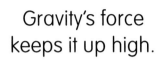

Gravity's force
keeps it up high.

There was an old astronaut who swallowed a planet.
It tasted like granite when she swallowed that planet.

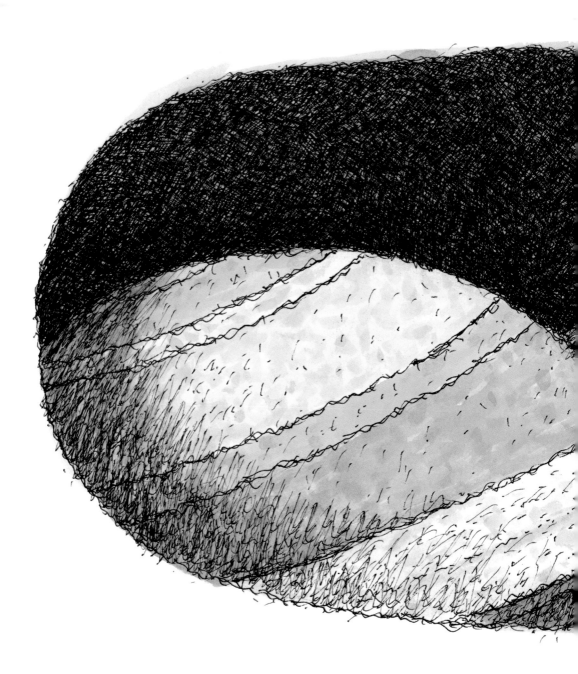

She swallowed the planet to orbit the star.

She swallowed the star to shoot for the moon.

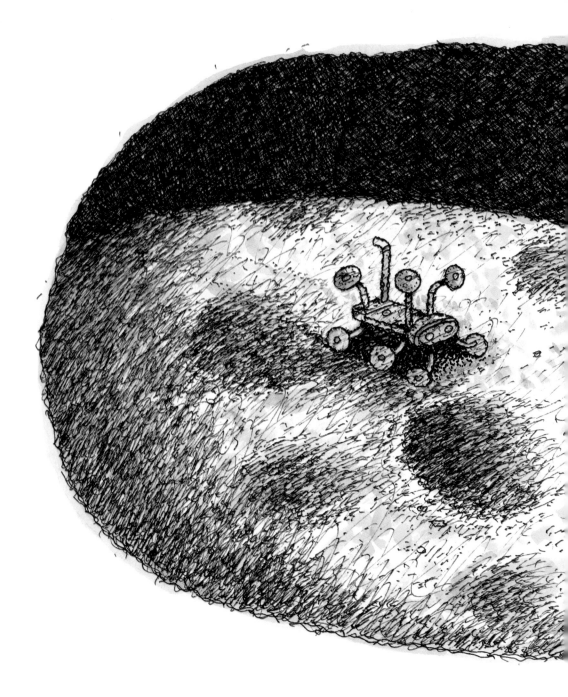

I don't know why she swallowed the moon.

It happened at noon.

The star closest to Earth is the sun.

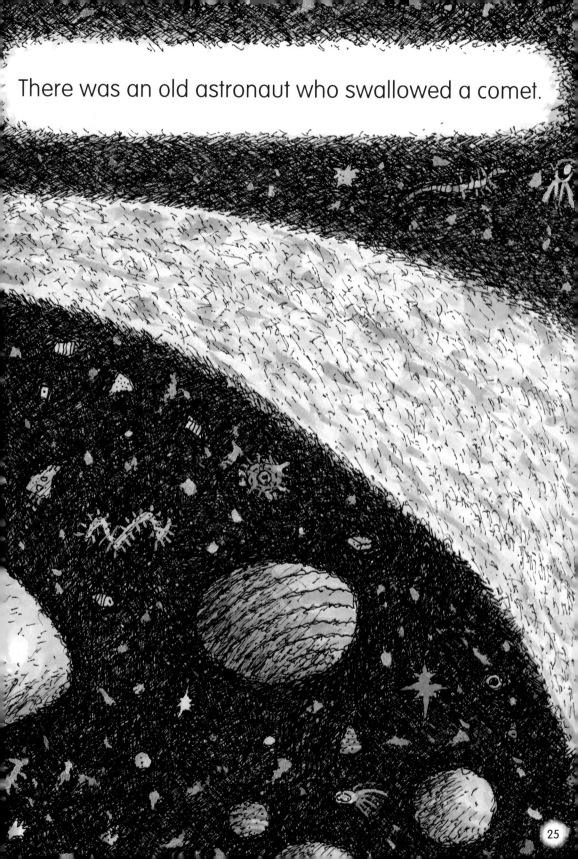

There was an old astronaut who swallowed a comet.

Just like an omelette, she swallowed that comet.

She swallowed the comet to light up the planet.
She swallowed the planet to orbit the star.

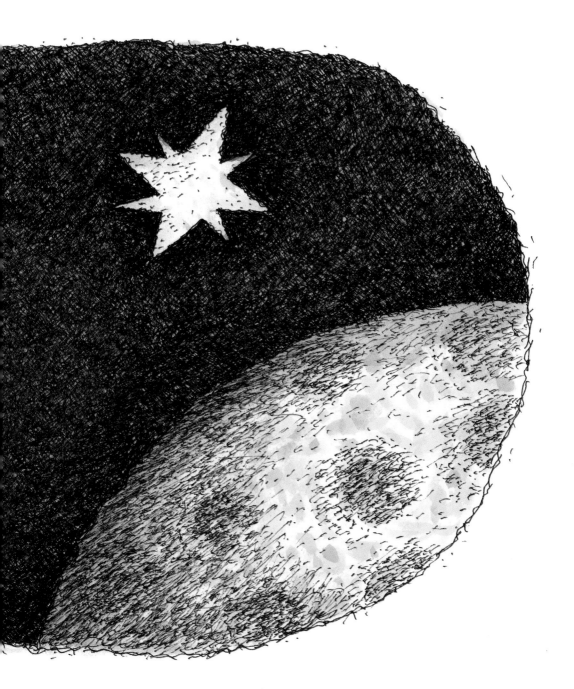

She swallowed the star to shoot for the moon.

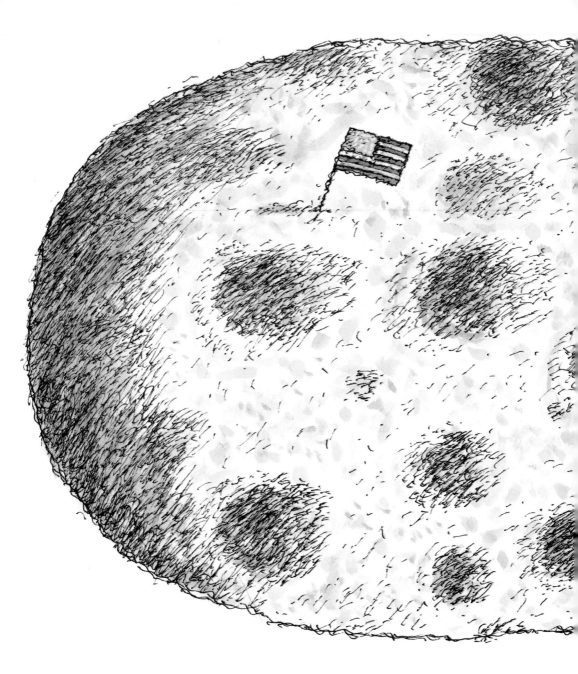

I don't know why she swallowed the moon.

It happened at noon.

There was an old astronaut who swallowed a meteoroid.
She really enjoyed that meteoroid.

She swallowed the meteoroid to fly with the comet.
She swallowed the comet to light up the planet.

She swallowed the planet to orbit the star.

She swallowed the star to shoot for the moon.

I don't know why she swallowed the moon.
It happened at noon.

There was an old astronaut who swallowed a rocket.
It was next on the docket, a powerful rocket.

She swallowed the rocket to catch the meteoroid.
She swallowed the meteoroid to fly with the comet.

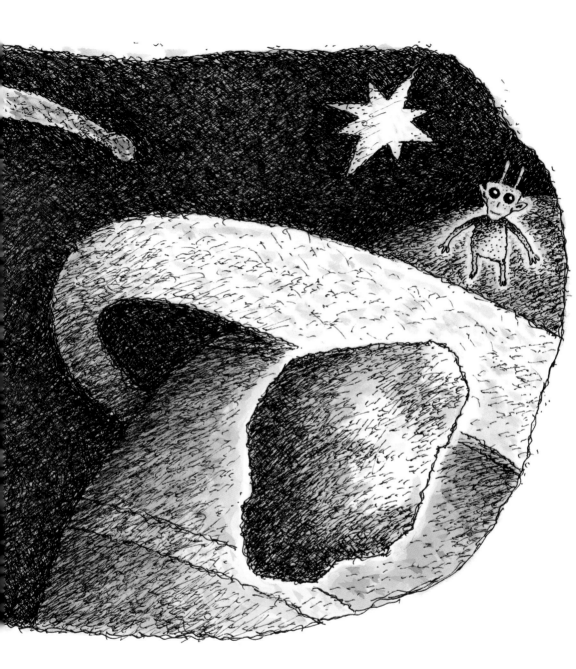

She swallowed the comet to light up the planet.
She swallowed the planet to orbit the star.

She swallowed the star to shoot for the moon.

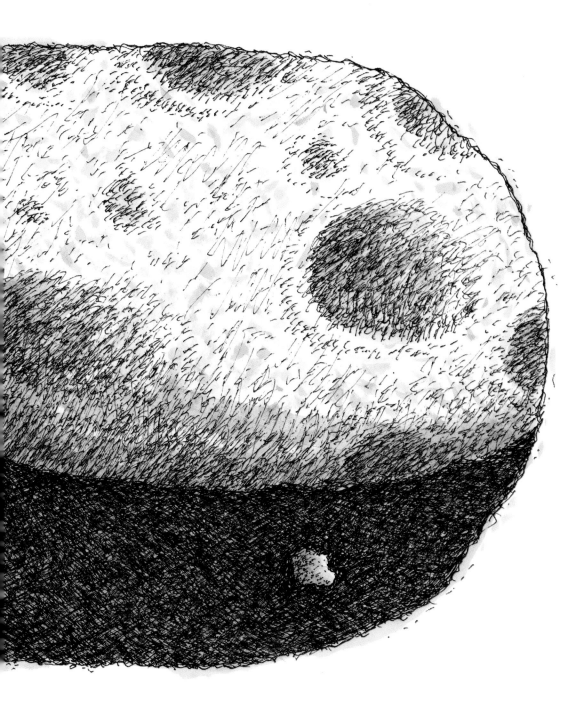

I don't know why she swallowed the moon.
It happened at noon.

There was an old astronaut who
swallowed a satellite.
It went down just right, that bright satellite.

There was an old astronaut who wanted to fly,
and spent all her time looking up high . . .

. . . at the planetarium's brightly lit sky.

The **moon** is Earth's closest neighbor, but it is still 238,855 miles away. It is the brightest object in the night sky because part of it faces the sun and it reflects the sun's light. The moon orbits Earth; it takes about 27 days for it to go all the way around. As the moon travels around Earth, it looks like it is changing shape, but it isn't. As it moves, the sun lights up the part of the moon facing the sun. These different shapes are the phases of the moon.

A **star** is a huge round ball of very hot gas. It is about fifty times hotter than boiling water. Stars don't really twinkle. When light from a star enters our atmosphere, the wind and temperature affect how we see the brightness and position of the star. That's why it looks like it's twinkling. The stars that you see in the night sky are only a small fraction of the more than billions of stars that exist in the universe.

Planets are natural objects that orbit around stars. Our solar system has eight planets: Mercury, Venus, Earth, Mars, Jupiter, Saturn, Uranus, and Neptune. These planets orbit around a star, our sun. Mercury has no moon because of its low gravity. Venus is the hottest planet in the solar system. Mars is the only planet, except for Earth, that has polar ice caps. Jupiter has 79 moons! Four of them were discovered by Galileo in 1610. Saturn has rings of ice surrounding it, but Neptune is actually the coldest planet. It takes Neptune about 165 Earth years to orbit the Sun. One year on Uranus equals 30,687 Earth days!

Comets are balls of ice and dust. They are very rare and orbit in very distant parts of space. When they orbit closer to the sun, the heat from the sun creates streams of gas that we see as a "tail." One of the most famous comets is Halley's Comet, which returns to Earth about every 75 years. You'll have to wait until 2061 to see it.

A **meteoroid** is a piece of rock, metal, or ice flying in space. A meteoroid that burns up as it passes through Earth's atmosphere is known as a meteor. We commonly call meteors shooting stars. Meteors are bits of rocks and ice ejected from comets as they move in their orbits about the sun. When hundreds of meteors speed across the night sky at the same time, we see a meteor shower. When a piece of meteoroid lands on Earth, it is called a meteorite.

Rockets are the vehicles that launch or move spacecraft into orbit. Rockets travel at least 25,000 miles per hour to reach the moon and planets. The rocket engine burns fuel that turns into gas. As the gas leaves the back of the rocket, the power moves the rocket forward. Think of letting the air out of a balloon. As the air escapes, the balloon moves in the opposite direction.

A **satellite** is any object that orbits another bigger object. There are natural satellites and man-made satellites. Earth orbits the sun, so it is a natural satellite. The moon is a natural satellite because it orbits Earth. Man-made satellites are launched into space to complete certain jobs. Weather satellites help us understand climate and also predict weather changes. Global Positioning System (GPS) satellites help you with directions. Satellites affect everyday life.

Search and Find!

Outer space is full of objects that scientists have studied, like stars, planets, and comets. But it's also full of lots of mysterious things we haven't even discovered yet! Go back through the story and see if you can find all the mystery objects in space before the old astronaut swallows them! When you've found them all, check your answers with the answer key at the bottom.
Happy searching!

Sun

Telescope

Glasses

Big Dipper

Empty spacesuit

Milky Way

Alien

UFO

American flag

Asteroid

Food tray

Chair

Flashlight

Camera

Test tubes

Rover

Solar panels

Rope

Jet pack

Walkie-talkie